Best of
Tenali Raman

© 2002 TINY TOT PUBLICATIONS
This Edition:-2002

Retold & Edited by: Shyam Dua

Published By:

TINY TOT PUBLICATIONS

235, Jagriti Enclave,
Vikas marg,
Delhi-110092 (INDIA)
Ph.: 216 7314, 216 3582,
Fax:- 91-11-2373023
email: tinytotpub@indiatimes.com

ISBN 81-7573-585-6

Printed at : HAPLOOS New Delhi.

Illustrated by
Aakriti Features, Delhi

CONTENTS

Tenali Meets Krishnadeva Raya

Here is a popular tale of how Tenali Raman came to be a jester in King Krishnadeva Raya's court.

It is said that Tenali Raman earned his name from the village he lived in. His true name was Ramakrishna and he lived in a village called Tenali. As a young Brahmin, Tenali Ramakrishna was a great devotee of Kalkidevi. He had great devotion in her. Once he prayed her for a whole night. She pleased and appeared to him. She directed him to meet King Krishnadeva Raya and to be jester in his court.

Tenali Raman visited Vijaynagar. He entered the royal court without permission and interrupted a dance performance. King Krishnadeva Raya became very angry. He ordered his guards to chop off Tenali Raman's head. He was put in prison for the night. He was to be killed in the morning. But witty Tenali's brain was already at work. Next morning the guards came to take him out of the cell for the execution. Tenali addressed them, "Dear friends, I am a Brahmin. I would like to follow the customs correctly. Please let me bathe in Tungabhadra river before I die."

The guards allowed Tenali Raman to do so. After a bath Tenali Raman sat by the riverside to meditate. Just as the guards got ready to do their duty, he said, "Please let me have some food after the bath and prayer."

The guards agreed to this request, too. They offered him coconuts and fruits to eat. After eating the food, the Brahmin got ready for a short nap. The guards were very surprised to see the requirements made by the fearless Brahmin. But, as a rule to fulfil the last wish of the accused, they were bound to agree with him. They allowed him to do so. But Tenali Raman, the Brahmin, slept for a few hours and the guards could not kill him. When he woke up, he asked innocently, "Oh, guards ! Why haven't you executed me yet ? You

must do as your king says. Let me make it easy for you. I'll just go and stand in the river neck deep. I'll shut my eyes and take Lord Rama's name. Then you can use your swords to cut off my neck."

So as arranged, he stood in water and said loudly, "Jai Shri Rama !". The moment he said the last word, he dived deep under water so the guard's sword cut through air. He appeared a few yards away in water. Then he asked to be taken to the king.

When the guards brought Tenali Raman to the king and narrated what had happened, the king smiled to himself. In his heart, he appreciated

Tenali Raman's wit and intelligence but he did not show it. He ordered the guards to let Tenali Raman be killed by elephants. The king waited to see how the intelligent Brahmin would escape this time.

The guards took Tenali Raman to the outskirts of the city. They dug a trench and buried Tenali Raman upto his neck and then filled up the trench. Then they left to get the elephant. Tenali Raman looked around for a way to escape. He saw a washerman with a hunch approaching him. He had a big bundle of clothes on his back. The washerman asked Tenali Raman what he was doing buried in the trench neck deep. Tenali Raman explained, "Friend, I am a washerman like you. I also developed a hunch like yours by carrying loads of clothes. A great vaidya told me to bury myself in this mud. Slowly and slowly my back-bone has straightened now."

The washerman believed Tenali Raman's fake tale

and wished to be cured of his hunched back, too. So he dug out the mud and freed Tenali Raman and got himself buried in his place. As the washerman was taking the bundle of clothes to the palace, Tenali assured him of delivering them at the palace.

Now the washerman lay buried in the trench neck deep in mud. When he saw guards leading an elephant in his direction, he started calling for help. His cries of help were noticed by the guards. They noticed that it was someone else in place of Tenali Raman. They freed the washerman and rushed to the palace to inform the king of the recent escape of Tenali.

On reaching the court the guards were surprised to see Tenali Raman in the presence of the king. He was narrating his tale of escape and the king and the courtiers were having a hearty laugh. The king then said, "Tenali Ramakrishna, you are indeed a clever man. You are hereby appointed a minister in my court."

But Tenali Raman said, "Your Majesty, I want to be a jester. I do not want to be a royal minister."

The king grew furious. He shouted, "You thankless

fellow, how dare you deny the royal orders! Go away. Don't you dare to show me your face ever again."

Tenali Ramakrishna bowed low and left the royal court. Next morning the royal court was held as everyday. Just then the courtiers saw a strange sight. A person was wearing clothes as all ministers do but he had his face covered with a large earthen pot. Two tiny holes in it helped him to see through the pot.

The king saw him, too, and enquired, "Who are you? What are you doing in this strange get up ?"

"Your Majesty, I am your royal jester."

"There are no jesters in my court," the king said.

"Actually I am one of your ministers. Yesterday you told never to show you my face, so I am here but you cannot see my face."

Actually it was Tenali Raman. Seeing and hearing all this, the king and the courtiers burst out laughing. The king embraced the intelligent Brahmin and so Tenali Ramakrishna was appointed as a royal jester in the royal court of Vijaynagar.

God in the Mirror

Tenali Raman was a great writer of funny poems. He attached to the court of Krishnadeva Raya of Vijaynagar kingdom.

One day, during a conversation, Tenali Raman declared to the king, "Your Majesty, people always like to lie whenever they get a chance to."

"How can you say that ! Tenali I have been a king for so many years but I have never lied. As far as I know, people lie under certain situations. They do not lie always as you said."

"Your Majesty, I have a point that there is no one in the world who has never·lied."

"Tenali, you are generalising. I, being a king, have never and can never lie."

"I can prove otherwise, Your Majesty."

"If so, then I challenge you," the king said.

"Your Majesty, I need a thousand gold coins and a year's time to prove my theory to you."

Thus, King Krishnadeva Raya agreed. After taking the money, Tenali did not appear in the court for a whole year. He engaged himself in constructing a large, palatial and beautiful house. Its interiors were colourful and attractive. The house had a room with a large mirror affixed to a wall. The other walls were adorned by beautiful paintings.

At last, a great and a beautiful house was ready. After a year, Tenali disguised himself as a sage. He went to King Krishnadeva Raya's court. No one, not even the king, could identify him. The sage approached the king and said, "Your Majesty, I have built a beautiful house for myself. I stay and pray there. My devotion has impressed God. He appears to me everyday in one of the rooms. I request you to feel free to see God for yourself. But he is only visible to those who lead a righteous life and have never lied in their lives."

King Krishnadeva Raya agreed to visit the sage's house. To test the sage's words, the king first sent a minister into the house. The minister admired the beautiful house and then reached the room fitted with the mirror. When he stood before the mirror, he saw his own reflection. He did not see any God. Now he was afraid to tell the truth to the king. He came out of the house and lied. He said, "Your Majesty, the sage is correct. I saw the God in the wall. I am so overwhelmed with emotions."

To confirm once more, the king asked another minister to go in. The second minister also saw his own reflection. He did not see God but was not courageous enough to tell the truth. He, too, came out and lied.

"Oh, Your Majesty! It was a glorious experience. I have no words to describe the experience exactly."

Now the king thought, "Hmm, Now I must go and check the truth" so the king went to the sage's home and when the king stood before the mirror, he, too, was faced by his own reflection. At this, he thought, "According to the sage, only a person, who has never lied, can see God in this wall. Now if I tell them 'I did not see God", they'll think that I am a liar."

The king went out of the room. He went to the sage and said, "You were right, sir. I saw God in that wall of the room. I am feeling so blessed."

"Your Majesty, are you sure you saw the God ?" asked the sage.

"Yes, I did," the king replied.

"You see God in that wall of the room, didn't you ?" the sage asked again.

The king replied positively yet the sage posed the same question again. This angered the king. He said, "How dare you suspect my answer ? If you were not a holy person then I would have never forgive you."

The sage smiled and pulled off his false beard. Tenali Raman now stood before the king. He said, "Your Majesty, you had insisted and I had believed that you as a king would never lie. Your Ministers were liars but you, too, behaved like them. Now do you accept that everyone is a liar sometime or the other."

Krishnadeva Raya accepted his defeat and felt ashamed of his conduct.

The Death Penalty Threat

Thattachari was the Rajguru in King Krishnadeva Raya's court. He was jealous of the favoured position held by Tenali Raman. Every time he could get a chance, he would falsely complain about Tenali to the king. The king in anger would announce the death penalty for Tenali Raman. But, due to his intelligence and quick wit, Tenali had been able to save his own skin.

One day Tenali Raman made a plan to get rid of the death penalty threat forever. He went to Thattachari and said, "Sir, a beautiful dancer has come to the city. She would like to meet a great man such as you because she has heard a lot about you. You must go to meet her tonight at the house where she is staying. She does not want you to get a bad name so she has asked you to come dressed as a woman."

Thattachari agreed to do so. Tenali then went to King Krishnadeva and told the same tale. The king had many wives and thought of acquiring another one. So he, too, agreed to dress up as a woman to meet the dancer.

That evening Tenali put off the lights of that house where he had called the Rajguru and the king.

Thattachari arrived first and sat in the darkened room. As he waited, he heard the sound of anklets. He saw a woman entered the room. Due to the dark, Thattachari could not see her face properly. The other woman was actually the king. Both of them took each other to be the dancer and waited for the other to begin the conversation. After moments of silence, Thattachari spoke up.

"My dear, why don't you show your beautiful face to me?"

he said in a gruff male voice.

The king recognised his voice and said, "Rajguruji! What is going on here? What are you doing here?"

The Rajguru recognised the king's voice at once. Both of them realized that Tenali had made a fool of them. As both tried to get out of the darkened room Tenali locked the door from outside and shouted from the window. "I'll let both of you go if you promise never to threaten me with death penalty again."

In that situation, they were helpless in the dark room. King and the Rajguru had no opinion but to agree to Tenali's words.

The Promoted Barber

The royal barber's only task was to give King Krishnadeva Raya his daily shave. One day when he arrived to do his job, King Krishnadeva Raya was still asleep. The barber gave him a shave even as he slept. On waking up, the king marvelled at the barber's skill of shaving a sleeping man. The king was pleased and told the barber to ask for anything of his choice. To this, the barber said, "Your Majesty, I would like to serve you as a minister in the royal court."

The king agreed to the barber's wish. As news

of the barber's promotion spread around, the other ministers became worried. They thought that an uneducated person at a minister's post may misuse the powers he held. They went to Tenali with the problem. Tenali assured them of his help.

The next morning when the king went for a stroll by the river, he was surprised to see Tenali scrubbing hard bathing a black dog. When the king asked what he was doing, Tenali replied, "Your Majesty, I am merely trying to convert a black dog into a white one by scrubbing it hard just as an unmodulated barber took post of the minister."

On hearing this, the king realized what Tenali was hinting at. That day, in the court, he appointed the barber back to his original position.

Choose Your Death

Once Tenali Raman received a stranger as a guest at his doorstep. He claimed to be his lost relative from his home town.

Tenali could not remember having seen him but let him stay as a guest in his house.

Suddenly one day due to some urgent work, Tenali had to leave for another town for the few days. Actually the stranger was none other than a spy from a neighbouring kingdom of vijaynagar. He had come to Vijaynagar with the intention of killing the king. Now in Tenali's absence he got a golden chance to carry out his plan. The stranger sent a fake note to the king in the hand-writing of Tenali's wife.

The king got the note. It read, "Your Majesty, I am feeling very ill. As my husband is out of town, I need your help and some medical attention."

On reading the note, the king rushed to Tenali's house with the royal vaidya and some assistants. The spy was hiding and waiting for the king's arrival. As soon as the king stepped into the Tenali's house, the spy pounced on him with a knife to stab him. But the alert king nabbed the attacker and saved himself.

After all this was over, the king was very angry at Tenali for harbouring a spy. On his return, the king called him in the royal court. When Tenali Raman reached the court, the king said, "Tenali Raman, It is a matter of shame. You let a spy stay in your house. He intended to kill me. For this you will be executed. Tell me how do you want to meet your death?"

"Your Majesty," Tenali said with a smile, "I wish to meet death by old age."

Hearing this, the king and all the courtiers burst out laughing at such a witty remark.

Burden of Debt

Due to some financial problem, Tenali Raman once borrowed some money from King Krishnadeva Raya.

Soon the time passed and the time for paying back the amount came near. But clever Tenali had no plans to give back the money as he always did with other creditors. He decided on a witty plan to escape paying back the amount.

One day the king received a note from Tenali's wife. It said that Tenali was very ill. As Tenali had not come to the court for many days, the king decided to visit him personally. In his mind, he had his suspicion that may be Tenali was upto something to avoid paying back the money.

The king reached Tenali's house. There he was lying on a bed covered up in a blanket. Seeing his sorry state the king asked his wife for the reason.

She said, "Your Majesty, he is under the burden of debt from you. The worry has eaten into his organs and he has fallen ill."

The king sympathised with Tenali and said, "Tenali, don't worry now. You are no longer bound to pay the debt. Stop worrying, relax and get well soon."

By listening these words, Tenali jumped out of the bed and smiled broadly at the king. He exclaimed, "Oh! I thank you, Your Majesty!"

"What is this, Tenali?

That means you were not ill! How dare you pull a lie on me!" the king grew angry.

"No, No, I did not lie, Your Majesty! I was ill under the burden of debt. Now that you have lifted the burden, I am hale and hearty."

As always, King Krishnadeva Raya had nothing to say but he smiled at witty Tenali's plan.

Tenali and the Thieves

Once many incidents of theft took place in Vijaynagar. Everyone was alert to the presence of thieves. One night, before retiring to bed, Tenali saw some movements in the bushes near his house. He was sure that some thieves were hiding there.

Tenali went into the house and made a plan with his wife. After a while, the thieves outside heard Tenali's loud voice. He was saying to his wife, "Dear wife, always remain careful. Keep the doors and windows of the house closed. I have heard that the robberies are taking place in the city. I fear for our precious jewels. I have put all of them in this large box. Help me carry it to the well behind our house in the garden. We'll throw it into the well. The thieves can never get to them this way."

The thieves heard all of this. Soon they saw Tenali and his wife dragging a large box to the well. They threw the box into the well. Then the couple went into their house and closed all the doors and windows.

The thieves were delighted at the golden chance. There were two of them. Both of them got busy taking out the water from the well to get at the box. They were busy for the whole night. By dawn they were very tired indeed but they had not got the box.

Early at dawn, Tenali came to the well. The thieves were very tired by drawing water for the whole night. When they saw Tenali approaching them, they began to run away. Smiling at them, Tenali said, "Oh! Thank you my friends, for watering my plants in the garden. What must I pay you for your labour ?"

Hearing this, the thieves fell at Tenali's feet begging for forgiveness. He let them go when they promised not to steal or rob anyone ever again.

A Cow for a Cat

Once many rats infested Vijaynagar. As a solution King Krishnadeva Raya announced that each family would be given a cat to catch the rats. So as not to burden the family with cat's care, the king also gave one cow to each family. The cows' milk was to be fed to the cats in the houses.

Tenali Raman did not relish this silly suggestion. He made a plan to make the king realize his folly.

Daily Tenali Raman served hot boiling milk to the cat in his house. As the cat sipped the hot milk, it burnt its tongue badly. So it stopped drinking the milk.

One day the king went around the city for the

inspection of the house cats. At everyone's house he saw a healthy cat but Tenali's cat was thin and weak. On enquiring, Tenali said that the cat was not drinking the milk. To confirm this, the cat was offered milk in the presence of the king but the memory of the burnt tongue made the cat run away on seeing the bowl of milk. The king thought for a moment and realized what Tenali must have done to the cat. He became angry and asked his guards to give Tenali a hundred lashes.

Tenali Raman did not protest at all. He faced the king and said, "I don't mind bearing the lashes. I still think that it's a waste to feed fresh milk to cats when humans are not getting enough milk for themselves."

Hearing these logical words of Tenali, King Krishnadeva Raya realized the foolishness of his plans. He announced that the cows' milk could be used by the people and the cats happily survived on the rats.

The Culprit

One day king and his courtiers were attending the royal court. Tenali Raman was also present there. Suddenly a shepherd came there with a plea. The shepherd said, "Your Majesty, I have come to seek justice. Please help me."

"Tell me what happened with you ?" asked the king.

"Your majesty, there lived a miser in my neighbourhood. His house is very old but he does not gets it repaired. Yesterday one of the walls of his house collapsed. My goat crushed under the wall and died. Please help me to get compensation money."

But Tenali Raman got up from his seat and said, "Your Majesty, I don't think the neighbour can be blamed for the wall collapse."

"Then, in your opinion, who is to blame ?" asked the king.

"Your Majesty, if you give me some time I'll get at the bottom of this case and find the real culprit." Tenali replied.

The king agreed to Tenali Raman's suggestion. Tenali Raman summoned the shepherd's neighbour and asked him to compensate for the crushed goat. The neighbour said, "I am not to blame for this. It was the mason who built this wall. Perhaps it had not been built strong enough, so it collapsed."

Tenali Raman then called for the mason. The mason declared, "Sir, I am not concerned with this. It was the labourer who mixed a thin watery batter of cement which could not hold up the bricks in the wall. You must ask him to pay up."

The king sent his guards to call the labourer. On arrival before the king, the labourer declared, "Sir, I cannot take the blame for this. It was the water man who poured the extra water in the mortar. He must be caught and made to compensate the shepherd."

The water man was called for. Hearing the blame, he said, "It's not my fault sir. The water-carrier, I use is very big. You must get hold of the man who gave me such a big water-carrier that holds more water than the measured amount required."

Tenali Raman asked the store-keeper to tell him who had given the water-carrier to him. He pointed to the shepherd and said, "Sir, this shepherd had given the water-carrier to me which held so much water."

Tenali Raman then addressed the shepherd, "Look now, it's all your fault. Your wrong step led to the loss of your goat."

The shepherd left the court with a shamed face. The king and the courtiers could not help but smile at witty Tenali Raman's sense of justice.

The Priest's Challenge

Once a learned priest and scholar visited King Krishnadeva Raya's court. He bowed to the king and said, "Your Majesty, I have heard that many learned people are present here in your court. I have come to confirm this. I will pose a question and anyone present in the court is free to answer it."

The king said, "Learned sir, our Rajguru is a great scholar, too. He will answer your questions.

The priest asked, "How can you say that this world is nothing but a false thing-a maya ?"

To this, the Rajguru replied, "Well, it is written in the Shastras and the Shastras are correct. Nothing in them is a lie."

"How can you say that whatever is in the Shastras is true ? Just prove to me through discussion and logic that this world is just maya."

The Rajguru said, "When a child is born, he is naked, not even a single piece of cloth covers him. He comes into the world with no belongings at all. When he dies, he goes from this world but takes nothing from here. The luxuries and possessions are all false, for a small period of time. It's all maya."

"No, sir! You are giving me a philosophical argument. I want a practical and logical discussion." said the scholar.

The king looked at Tenali Raman. He got up from his seat and said, "Sir, I'll give you a logical and practical explanation. Tell me where are the Himalayas ?"

"To the North of India ?" the scholar replied.

"If you were in Tibet, where would the Himalayas be ?"

"To the South of the country," the priestly scholar said.

"So what is true for you may be a lie or a false for one in Tibet. During day time you will say its daytime but, far away in a western country, it is night time. For the people living in that country, you are lying or what you claim is false. What is true for one is false for another. This way everything and everyone is lying and all is false around us. Thus, as you wanted to prove this whole world is maya, a false belief, something always changing and never the same. So I have proved what you wanted."

The priest had no reply to give and, thus, Tenali Raman again saved the grace of Vijaynagar.

The Honest One

Once a heated discussion was going on in King Krishnadeva Raya's court. The Rajguru claimed, "Your Majesty, if compared to the rich, the poor people are more dishonest. It's not that they are dishonest by nature. They are dishonest due to the poverty conditions that they have to live in."

But Tenali Raman disagreed. To prove his point he asked the king to give him two small bags full of money and a week's time. The king agreed. Tenali Raman knew that every morning a rich merchant used to pass on a path by the river Narmada. He used to go there for a dip in the river. On the same path a poor man used to pass by everyday as he used to go to look for work. Tenali Raman dropped the two bags on that path. He went and told this to the king and both of them waited for the bags to be returned.

The next morning the rich merchant found the bag full of gold coins. He took it and thought, "Oh ! What luck ! Goddess Lakshmi has blessed me today." He went back home and hid the gold coins.

A while later the poor man came down the path and saw a bag lying there. He opened it and found gold coins in it. He thought, "Oh ! So much wealth ! I wonder who owns this bag. He must be so worried at having loss of it. I must give it to the royal treasurer."

So the poor man went to the royal treasury and deposited the bag of gold coins. He took a receipt from the treasurer.

A week went by and Tenali Raman went to the king and said, "Your Majesty, only one of the bags of gold coins has been received. It was the poor man who deposited it."

The poor man and the rich merchant were summoned in the royal court. The king asked the rich merchant, "Where is the bag of gold coins you found in the path?"

"Your Majesty," said the merchant. "I invested that money in my business but I suffered a great loss."

"Why did you take the bag which did not belong to you ?" asked the king.

"Your Majesty, I took that wealth as a blessing from the Goddess Lakshmi."

Then the king asked the poor man, "Why did you deposit the money in the royal treasury ? You are poor and you could have utilised it well."

"Yes, Your Majesty, that's true but my conscience did not allow me to keep what is not mine. I thought maybe it belonged to someone who was more in need of it than I was. I did not want to sin by taking what was not mine."

Hearing this, Tenali Raman said, "Your Majesty, did I not tell you that a poor man will be honest but not a rich man ?"

The king and the courtiers agreed with Tenali Raman and the Rajguru just hung his head in disappointment.

The Tinkle of Coins

One day a very old man reached King Krishnadeva Raya's court. He was walking with the help of a stick and had tears in his eyes. In a pleading tone, he addressed the king, "Your Majesty, help me and solve my problem. My son and daughter-in-law have shut me out of the house. They don't even feed me. They keep taunting me, where can an old man like me go to stay ?"

"Don't worry now," said the king " I'll summon your son to the court and ask him to treat you more respectfully ever after. After all you are his father."

After the old man left reassured, Tenali Raman said, "Your Majesty, I wants to handle that case so that the old man's son and daughter-in-law will serve him with great regards for the rest of his life".

The king allowed Tenali Raman to do what he wanted. Tenali Raman said, "Thank you, Your Majesty. You'll see that in a day or two, the old man will come to you in a better and happy state of mind."

That day Tenali Raman went and met the old man at a secret place. He asked him to come to the court after two days.

As Tenali Raman had said, the old man appeared in the court after two days. The king enquired, "So, how are your son and daughter-in-law treating you now?"

"Now I am very happy, Your Majesty. They are busy serving me all day long. They give me delicious dishes to eat and press my feet as I lie down to rest." replied the old man.

"Oh! It means the fear of a royal rebuke made them change their behaviour towards you!"

"No, Your Majesty! Actually they don't even know that I had met you to complain about them. It was Tenali Raman's plan that did the trick."

The king asked Tenali to reveal the plan. Tenali promised to tell the king when they were alone, away from the courtiers. So, when the king met Tenali in his private chamber, Tenali said, "Your

Majesty, I gave the old man a large bag full of gold coins which I had saved for myself. I told him to count the gold coins when his son and daughter-in-law were not near him. I told him to act as if he was counting them in their absence to keep it hidden from their knowledge. I had asked him to do this for a day or two. Then he returned the gold coins to me secretly and kept the bag tied round his waist by a thin rope. This way his son and daughter-in-law thought that he had a lot of wealth hidden away. To gain this wealth, they will treat him well for the rest of his life."

"But what will happen when they will come to know the truth ?", the king asked Tenali.

"I don't think this will be revealed if the old man is careful enough and anyway he is very old. He won't live for many years now. Atleast he'll have a decent life just before death."

The king praised Tenali Raman for his intelligent plan that helped the poor man.

Tenali Raman in Dilli Durbar

At the time when Krishnadeva Raya ruled over vijaynagar, King Babar ruled over Delhi. Tenali Raman was a famous jester in King Krishnadeva Raya's royal court. When King Babar heard Tenali's tales of wit and intelligence, he wished to meet him. So he sent a messenger to Vijaynagar to request Tenali Raman to visit Delhi. With King Krishnadeva Raya's permission Tenali Raman went to Delhi with the messenger.

In Delhi, Tenali was welcomed and settled in the royal guest house. The messenger went to King Babar to inform him about Tenali's arrival. The next day's appointment was fixed between King Babar and Tenali Raman. Babar told his courtiers, "Tenali Raman, the great witty jester from Vijaynagar has come to Delhi. Tomorrow in the royal court none of you must smile or laugh at his jokes. I want to test him as to how he will make us laugh and win a reward."

The courtiers of Dilli Durbar promised not to smile or laugh that day in the court before the guest. At the given time Tenali Raman also arrived in Dilli Durbar. He told many witty tales and jokes but courtiers and King Babar, all remained silent. No one even smiled at the jokes. This went on everyday for fifteen days. From the sixteenth day, Tenali stopped going to Dilli Durbar. He disguised himself and followed King Babar everywhere to note his daily routine. Babar used to go for stroll by the river Yamuna with his Prime Minister every morning. On the way they would give gold coins to the poor and the needy beggars. After observing this, Tenali made a plan.

Next morning, Tenali Raman dressed up as an old man. He took a spade and a mango sapling and stood by the river Yamuna waiting for the King Babar's arrival. Seeing him at a distance, Tenali started planting the sapling. King Babar came to him and said, "Old man, you are very old indeed. You won't live long enough to enjoy the fruits of the tree you are planting. Why are you taking so much trouble?"

"Your Majesty, I enjoyed the fruits from the trees planted by my ancestors. This tree's fruits will be enjoyed by others. I find joy in giving to others. I am not planting this for myself."

The king was impressed by the reply. He gave the old man a bag full of gold coins. The old man thanked him and said,

"Your Majesty, you are indeed a great and kind king. People get the fruits when the tree has grown but you have given me the fruit of my labours even before I had planted the sapling. The thoughts of helping others has really benefitted me."

"I like this thought of yours. You can now take this second bag of gold coins as a reward," King Babar said. "Oh, Your Majesty ! I am overwhelmed," the old man sighed. "This tree will bear fruits once a year only but before it has been planted you have filled my arms with fruits of joys twice."

"I like your thoughts. I am impressed by them. Take this third bag of gold coins as a reward," said King Babar.

Now the Prime Minister got worried. He whispered to King Babar, "Your Majesty, let's leave now. This man is too intelligent. His witty remarks will surely claim all the royal wealth from you."

King Babar laughed aloud and got ready to walk away. At this the old man said, "Your Majesty, can you give me just a look ?"

When Babar turned to look, he saw Tenali Raman holding the false beard in his hands. King Babar burst out laughing on seeing what Tenali had been up to. He said, "I am very pleased, Tenali. You have truly proved that you are witty and a great jester, too."

King Babar called Tenali Raman to the court the next day and gave him many more royal rewards.

When Tenali Raman returned to Vijaynagar, King Krishnadeva Raya was proud to see how Tenali had saved grace. Tenali smiled and said, "So, Your Majesty, am I fit for a reward from you, too ?"

King Krishnadeva Raya agreed with a smile and gave Tenali ten thousand gold coins as reward.

Other's Faults

One day a courtier named Gun Sunder and the Rajguru got into an argument. Gun Sunder insisted, "Rajguruji, its easy to point out others faults but difficult to improve on them."

"I don't agree," the Rajguru claimed.

Tenali Raman had heard their arguments from a far. Just at that moment, a man entered the royal court. He bowed to King Krishnadeva Raya and said, "Your Majesty, I am a painter from Kalinga. I have brought a beautiful painting as a gift for you."

The king received the painting. It was of a beautiful woman. It seemed so real as if she would speak up at any moment. The king passed on the painting to his courtiers to see. But each of them found something wrong in the

painting; some thought the lady's nose was too small while others found fault with the lips. Thus, all the courtiers found fault with the painting. When it was Tenali's chance he said, "Your Majesty, I am not a great art critic. I suggest that you hang this painting at the cross-roads of the city and make an announcement that anyone can mark on the painting wherever they find a fault in the painting. Thus, you'll have critical comments and approval from the public."

King Krishnadeva Raya liked the suggestion. Soon the picture was hung on a pole at the city's cross-roads. People were free to make a mark on the painting where they saw a fault. The next day, when the king received back the painting, it was a mess. The markings had obscured the face of the lady in the painting.

Once again Tenali suggested, "Your Majesty, let the picture be hanged at the cross-roads once again and make an announcement that those who had marked the faults must now improve upon faults in the paintings. They will be suitably rewarded for this."

So the painting was hung at the cross-roads once again. But, inspite of the announced reward, no one came forward to rectify the faults which they had pointed out. When the painting was brought back to the king, he saw no changes made to it. Tenali Raman said, "Your Majesty, this is human nature. Everyone is ready to point out others' fault but never ready to put them right."

With these words, Tenali smiled at Gun Sunder. He understood that Tenali was supporting his view in the discussion with Rajguru. Rajguru felt ashamed at his defeat.

The king bought the painting anyway and rewarded both Tenali and the painter.

Tenali's Experiment

Due to his intelligence and wit, Tenali Raman was loved by every one. But the Rajguru was very jealous of him. He had some flatterer courtiers, too, who shared the same view. One day they all got together to make a plan to humiliate Tenali Raman. The next day in the royal court Rajguru told King Krishnadeva Raya, "Your Majesty, I have heard that Tenali has learnt to make Paras, a magical stone that can change iron into gold."

"Is that so ! If your information is true then, being the king, it is I who must get the Paras for the welfare of the people of my kingdom. I'll ask Tenali about it."

"But, Your Majesty, please don't tell him that you got this news from me." Rajguru pleaded and the king promised him that he wouldn't."

When Tenali Raman arrived in the court that day,

the king addressed him, "Tenali, I've heard that you have the Paras with you. You have accumulated a lot of gold by changing iron into it.

Tenali was intelligent hence he realized that someone had told a false tale to the king to plot against him. Therefore he pretended to please the king and said, "Yes, Your Majesty, it's true."

"Then you must show me your skill in the court here and now."

"Your Majesty, I cannot do so now. It takes some time and arrangements. Tomorrow morning, I'll show this experiment of changing iron into gold."

Now Rajguru and his supporters were sure that Tenali had been trapped for good.

Next day Tenali arrived in the court with a street dog. Its tail had been put into a pipe. Everyone who saw them, laughed aloud but the king got furious, "Tenali, how

48

dare you bring a street dog into the royal court?"

"Your Majesty, first you must clear my question. Do you know as everyone else does that even if a dog's tail is tied up in a straight pipe for several years, it stays the same. It won't leave its crooked character?"

"Yes, I know about this," the king agreed.

"But here, by doing this experiment, I want to prove otherwise," said Tenali Raman.

"Oh Tenali ! Don't act so foolishly. You know you'll never succeed in straightening a dog's crooked tail. It isn't in its nature."

"That's exactly what I want to show. When a dog's tail cannot be mended against its true nature, how can iron leave its natural characteristic to change into gold ?"

King Krishnadeva Raya realized that he had been blindly led to believe the Rajguru's words. He did not say anything to the Rajguru but rewarded Tenali Raman for his cleverness. Which was punishment and humiliation enough for Rajguru and his supporters.

Judging by Appearance

The Chief of army in Vijaynagar kingdom begot a son. He invited the king and the courtiers for a feast on that occasion. On the appointed day, the king and the courtiers arrived to bless the newborn and to eat the sweets. The king approached the infant in the cradle and said, "God bless you child ! May you be a great warrior like your father."

Tenali Raman went to the cradle and said, "Your Majesty, he will be a greater warrior than his father. I can tell by the look of the baby."

The incident was forgotten by the king but the jealous courtiers saw another chance to humiliate Tenali. One of them said to the king, "Your Majesty, Tenali Raman had made the comments to insult your intelligence. How can he tell what the baby will grow up to be ?"

"You are right. I think we should test him. Can you suggest someway for this ?" The king enquired.

The courtier said, "Your Majesty, we'll order two identical gold vessels to be made. One must be of solid gold and the other must be of hollow gold. We'll tie the vessels by identical chains on the ceilings. Then we'll ask Tenali to look from a distance and, without touching it, he must identify which is hollow and which one solid."

King Krishnadeva Raya asked his

servants to arrange for this test. Thus, two identical gold vessels were hung by chains for Tenali to see and identify. Tenali Raman was summoned and asked to tell which was of hollow gold and which was of solid gold. He said, "Your Majesty, the one on the right is made of solid gold and the one on the left is made of hollow gold."

The king and the courtiers were surprised by Tenali's correct answer. The king asked him, "Tenali, how could you tell correctly by seeing from so faraway ?"

"Your Majesty, I observed and judged that the chain tied to one vessel was straining due to weight. The other vessel was hollow and light so that it was swaying slightly. I could therefore, judge that the strained chain held the solid gold vessel."

The king and the courtiers agreed with his experiment. The king said, "Tenali, this was to test if you were able to judge by appearance. I agree that you have this skill of judging correctly."

The Camel's Hump

Once King Krishnadeva Raya was very happy and impressed by Tenali Raman's witty talk. In his happy mood, he said, "Tenali, you have indeed pleased me today. Now I give to you, an entire town as a gift."

Tenali Raman bowed down thankfully. Many days went by but the king did nothing to keep his words. He had forgotten the promise of gifting a town to Tenali Raman. Tenali Raman felt it odd to remind the king of his words. He was always on the look out to remind the king of this.

One day an Arab paid a visit to Vijaynagar. He had a camel with him. A large crowd gathered to see the camel as they had not seen one but had only heard about it. King Krishnadeva Raya and Tenali Raman also went to see the strange animal.

As both of them stood looking at the camel, the king commented, "Camel is a strange animal indeed. It has such a long neck and two humps on its back. I wonder why the Lord created such a strange and ugly animal."

Tenali Raman got the chance he had been waiting for. As always he was ready with his witty reply. He said, "Your Majesty, I think, rather I am sure that the camel was a king in its previous birth. May be the king had promised someone to give a town and forgotten about his promise. As a punishment the Lord turned the king into this ugly animal."

Initially, the king took this to be just a witty tale of Tenali Raman's imagination. But a few minutes later, he realized that Tenali Raman had reminded him of the words he had not kept.

On his return to the royal palace the king promptly summoned his accountant. He asked him to give it in writing that he was gifting a town to Tenali Raman and the arrangements for the same would be carried out immediately.

Tenali Raman thanked the king for his generous favour. Thus once again Tenali Raman's wit came in handy to his benefit.

Tenali Raman Trains a Horse

Once King Krishnadeva
Raya had some horses
imported from Persia.
He gave one horse each to his cavalry men for
training them. Tenali Raman wished to have one,
too. The king agreed and gave a horse to him. To
everyone the king gave money to be spent on the
horses' training and upkeeping.

Tenali Raman took the horse and the money to his
house. Then he built a barn for the horse. But the
barn was closed from all sides. A small hole was
kept open to pass the hay through for the horse to
eat. A thin drain was dug and water was poured
into it for the horse to drink. The drain used to
reach a small corner of the barn. Tenali fed the
horse with hay at a given time in the day. He fed the
horse only once a day. The hungry horse would
snatch the hay as soon as it was passed through
the hole. Many days passed this way.

Then, one day the king decided to inspect the horses he had given for training. He saw well maintained, healthy horses with shiny eyes and cheerful nature. When they were set free, they galloped around gracefully. All the cavalry men and their horses were inspected and found well-groomed. But the king noticed that Tenali Raman and his horse were missing. When the king summoned Tenali Raman, he explained, "I wanted to be present at the horses' inspection, too. But my horse has become very stubborn. It is not coming out of the barn. I need some help to fetch it here."

The king called his guards to accompany Tenali Raman to the barn but he said, "Your Majesty, even though I have trained the horse but it's not obeying me, its master. When I, as its trainer, could not fetch it then how can these guards do that. I request you to send some scholarly and holy person for this task."

Actually, Tenali Raman said this because he was sure the king would send Subba Shastri. Subba

Shastri was a learned Purohit but he was jealous of Tenali Raman. Tenali Raman wanted to teach him a lesson. As expected the king did summon Subba Shastri to fetch Tenali Raman's horse. The king said, "Purohitji, you are a learned Brahmin. You know all the Shastras including Ashwashastra, the science of horses. Please go and help Tenali Raman."

Subba Shastri wanted to prove his superiority to Tenali Raman, so he readily agreed.

At the barn Tenali Raman said, "Purohitji, would you like to look at the special horse of mine ? Kindly look through the opening in the wall."

Subba Shastri eagerly peeped through the opening. His long, white beard appeared like hay to the horse inside. The horse soon held the Purohit's beard in his teeth in a tight grip. Subba Shastri could not pull back and his head was stuck in the opening. He howled in pain and anguish. Soon he started shouting for help.

"So Purohitji, has your knowledge of Shastras fetched the horse out yet ?" Tenali Raman asked with a smile. "Oh! Raman, help me please. My boastings were a mistake. Please forgive me."

After hearing the apologies, Tenali Raman asked his servants to break down the walls of the barn. The horse still held on to Subba Shastri's beard. Both of them were taken to the king in the same state with great difficulty. The king was surrounded by the horses and the cavalry men. The men broke out into laughters at the sight. At this sound, the horses neighed, too. In response to them, Tenali Raman's horse opened its mouth to neigh. Thus Subba Shastri's long beard was free from the horse's tight grip. Subba Shastri had learnt a lesson well never again to try and demean Tenali Raman.

When the king saw Tenali Raman's horse,

he saw it to be a weak as compared to other horses, because it had been fed only once in a day. The king enquired, "Tenali Raman, why is your horse so weak ? I had given you money for fodder to be fed to it."

"Your Majestry, this horse had become so stubborn after being fed for only once in a day. Can you imagine what it could have done to the Purohitji if I had fed it more like the others have done ?"

"But Tenali Raman, the way you have treated the great Purohitji is not respectable."

At this Subba Shastri intervened. He said, "Your Majesty, please do not say anything to Tenali Raman. I deserve the way I've been treated. I have teased and insulted him many times. Today I've learnt a lesson that, along with education, one must learn to respect and love others. He has taught me a lesson for life hence he is my guru."

With these words, Subba Shastri bowed to Tenali Raman. Tenali Raman bowed back and apologised. Thus, the matter was settled amicably.

Tenali Raman's Son

King Krishnadeva Raya's palace had a large royal garden. Beautiful and rare varieties of flowers grew there. Once a foreigner gifted him a creeper on which roses grew. Of all the flower plants in the garden, the king liked that creeper the most. One day the king noticed that the number of roses were decreasing on the creeper. He realized that the roses were surely being stolen. He ordered the watchmen to stay alert and catch the rose-thief.

Next day the watchman caught the thief red handed. He was none other than Tenali Raman's son. As was the custom, the thief was taken round the streets of Vijaynagar for all to see. Tenali Raman had heard that his son had been caught stealing the roses. As his son passed by the street near Tenali's house with the guards, Tenali's wife said, "Why don't you do something to save our son ?"

At this Tenali Raman spoke up loud enough for his son to hear. He said, "What can I do ? If he uses his sharp tongue maybe he can save himself."

When Tenali Raman's son heard this, he did not understand immediately.

A few minutes later, he realized what his father had meant. 'Using his sharp tongue' meant that 'he should eat up the sweet roses before anyone saw this'. So, by the time they reached the palace, he had eaten up all the roses and the guards had not noticed this.

In the royal court the guards presented Tenali Raman's son before the king and said, "Your Majesty, we caught this boy red handed as he was stealing the roses."

"Oh ! This small boy is a thief, is he ?" Said the king surprisingly.

Tenali Raman's son said, "Your Majesty, the guards could not catch the thief. I was passing by the garden and they caught me to impress you. Actually I think they are stealing the roses themselves. Can you see any flowers with me ? Shouldn't they be in my hands if I was caught red

handed ? Your Majesty, ask the guards where the rose flowers have gone."

The guards wondered on not finding the flowers. The king was furious at them. He said, "How could you call an innocent child a thief ? There is no evidence to prove it either. Go away and never accuse anyone without evidence ever again."

Thus, Tenali Raman's son was set free.

A Great Book

Once there came a great scholar to king Krishnadeva Raya's court. He claimed that no one could challenge the knowledge he possessed. He challenged all the learned scholar from the royal court to discuss any topic in debate with him. As his fame was well known, none of the royal scholars dared to accept the challenge. It became a tedious matter before the royal court of Vijaynagar. The scholars went to Tenali Raman and pleaded for help. Tenali Raman agreed to help them. A date for the debate was fixed.

On the appointed day, Tenali Raman arrived in the royal court disguised as a learned, scholarly priest. Under one of his arms, he held a large bundle which looked like it had voluminous books in it. Soon the great scholar came and sat opposite the priest. The priest bowed to the king, took the bundle from under his arms and placed it between himself and the scholar. Then they sat down for the debate.

The king knew that Tenali Raman as a priest surely had some plan in his mind. The king declared that the debate must begin.

Tenali Raman disguised as the priest, stood up from his seat and said, "Learned sir, I have heard much about you. For a great scholar like you, I have brought this great and rare book on which we will debate now."

"Sir, please name the book for I have read and know of all," the scholar said.

Tenali Raman said, "Learned sir, the book is called 'Tilakashta Mahisha Bandhana'."

The scholar was surprised. In all his life of gaining knowledge, he had never heard of any work with such a title. Now he was scared to debate on a book he had never read and heard of. Even so, he said, "Oh! That's a rare work indeed. It's been so many years since I read it. Let me read it tonight as I have forgotten many points in it. Tomorrow we'll debate on it after I have refreshed my memory."

Tenali Raman agreed to this easily. But that night the scholar fled the city as he feared humiliation on losing the debate.

Next morning when the scholar failed to come in the royal court, Tenali Raman said, "Your Majesty, the scholar will not come. He has left the city."

"Tenali, tell me now about the rare book you wanted to debate upon," asked King Krishnadeva Raya.

"Your Majesty, actually there is no such book. I had named it 'Tilakashta Mahisha Bandhana'. In this title, the word ' Tilakashta' means dried sticks of sesame. 'Mahisha Bandhana' means 'a rope' which is used to tie a buffalo. The bundle I was carrying were actually dried sesame sticks tied with a rope. I had wrapped it in silk so that it looked like a bundle of books."

Hearing this, the king and the courtiers could not control their laughter. The king was so impressed that he gave a reward to Tenali Raman.

The Special Dish

Once on the occasion of King Krishnadeva Raya's birthday a grand feast was held. All the invited guests and courtiers enjoyed the tasty dishes. After having his fill, Tenali Raman went home. There he said to his wife, "Dear, no doubt the king had arranged a wonderful feast. I really enjoyed a costly meal today. I ate a dish prepared of rare seedless brinjals and it was the best part of the meal. There was none to eat and praise that dish but I have never eaten anything so delicious in all my life!"

Tenali's wife said, "I think you are mistaken. There are no seedless brinjals in this world."

Tenali said to his wife, "No, no, I am very sure they were seedless brinjals. A foreigner gave the brinjal seeds as a gift to the king. They are specially grown in the royal kitchen-garden. They tasted very good in the thick curry."

"Oh ! The way you are describing them is making my mouth watered, too. Can you get the seedless brinjals for me, too ?"

"No, dear ! It's quite impossible. No one can pluck them without royal permission."

Tenali tried to quiten with his wife. But she was not ready to understand her husband. Finally she said, "Oh ! What a good luck I have ! Many many thanks to God who have given me such a husband that he cannot even fulfil such a simple request of mine. You are selfish man indeed."

Hearing such words, Tenali Raman agreed to get the seedless brinjals for his wife. He wrapped himself in his wife's black saree and went to steal the brinjals when it grew dark. He stealthily entered the royal kitchen-garden, plucked the brinjals and ran home. At home he gave the seedless brinjals to his wife. She cooked them eagerly. As she tasted the curry she loved the taste. She said to Tenali, "Dear, go and wake up our son. Let him taste the curry, too."

"No, don't wake him

up. He is a child. He'll go and tell everyone and thus, the king will know that I stole the brinjals."

But Tenali's wife did not agree to it. She forced Tenali Raman strongly to wake up his son. His son was sleeping in the open courtyard. Tenali Raman sprinkled some water on his son's face. Then he woke up his sleeping son and said, "Come on, son, it's raining, come inside." When his son stepped inside, Tenali's wife served the tasty curry to him.

Next day the king found out that someone had plucked seedless brinjals from the kitchen-garden. He became very angry. A jealous courtier said, "Your Majesty, it must be Tenali Raman for he was curious to know what the tasty curry was made of. He was told about the seedless brinjals and maybe he stole them."

Another courtier said, "Tenali will get penalty free if asked about it. We must ask his son if he ate that curry, for children never lie."

So Tenali Raman's son was summoned in the royal court. On his arriaval to the royal court, the king asked the boy, "Dear boy, what did you eat for dinner

last night?"

"Sir, we ate tasty brinjal curry," the boy answered.

Now the king and the courtiers were sure that Tenali Raman had stolen the seedless brinjals. The king called Tenali Raman and said, "Tenali, why did you steal the seedless brinjals ? I would have gifted them to you if you requested for them."

"Your Majesty, my son ate when he was sleepy. He had slept early in the evening and was woken up for dinner. How can you believe a sleepy child's words ?"

His son intervened and said, "That's true, Your Majesty. My father had woken me up as I slept in the courtyard when it had started raining yesterday."

At this all the courtiers laughed for, everyone knew that it had not rained last evening. The king, too, agreed that the boy was too sleepy at the time of incident and could not be trusted to answer correctly. So he was let off.

Then, when the king and Tenali Raman were alone, the king asked, "Tenali Raman, can you tell me who the thief is ?" Tenali Raman said, "I'll tell you who he is if you forgive him."

The king agreed and Tenali Raman told him the complete story. At this, the king laughed and forgave Tenali Raman. He gave him the reward intended for the one who caught the brinjal thief.

The Last Wish

King Krishnadeva Raya's mother had grown very old. Once she fell seriously ill and she felt that she would die soon. She wished to give mangoes to the Brahmins as donation. She loved mangoes and felt giving away what she loved the most, in her last days. She believed that it would earn her a place in the heaven. Sadly it was not the season for mangoes. The king's mother passed away without fulfilling her last wish.

The king called a learned Brahmin and asked how his mother's last wish could be fulfilled. The Brahmin said, "To help her soul rest in peace you must give away mangoes of solid gold. Those should be given to Brahmins on your mother's death anniversary."

So, on his mother's death anniversary, the king invited some Brahmins for a feast. Then he gave mangoes made of gold to each of them.

When Tenali Raman learnt about this, he realized that the Brahmins had taken advantage of the king's innocence and generosity. To teach the Brahmins a lesson, Tenali Raman made a plan.

The next day, Tenali Raman sent invitations to the Brahmins. It read that Tenali Raman wanted to give donation on his mother's death anniversary. The Brahmins felt that they would receive a lot at Tenali Raman's house as he was a royal jester and a rich man. The Brahmins accepted the invitation and went to Tenali Raman's house on the appointed day.

After performing the rites, the Brahmins were served with a delicious lunch. They were very happy to savour the delicacies served. After the lunch, they eagerly awaited what they would receive in the donation. As they waited impatiently, they saw Tenali Raman placing iron rods in the fire. On enquiring, Tenali Raman said, "My mother suffered from arthritis. On her death bed, she was in severe pain. She asked me to get some hot iron rods to place on her body's joints to get rid of the pain. But she breathed her last before I could heat the iron rods. Now, to rest her soul in peace, I shall do the same to you Brahmins as it was her last wish."

"How can this be?" A Brahmins exclaimed. "Who told you that branding our bodies with iron rods as your mother wished, will fulfill her last wish ? Whoever told you that was a liar."

"No, sir," Tenali Raman said. "He did not lie. If the king can give golden mangoes to rest his mother's soul in peace, why can't I do so for my mother ?"

At this, the Brahmins realized what Tenali Raman meant. So they said, "Please, Tenali, forgive us. We will give those

golden mangoes to you. Please let us go."

So Tenali Raman took the golden mangoes and let the Brahmins go. But the mean Brahmins told the king about this. The king became angry and called Tenali Raman. He said, "Tenali, if you wanted the golden mangoes, I could have given them to you. Why were you so greedy to take them from the Brahmins ?"

"Your Majesty, I am not greedy. In fact, I was merely controlling their greedy nature. If they could take the golden mangoes from you on the occasion of death anniversary of your mother, then why did they refuse the donation of hot iron rods given on the same occasion by me ?"

King Krishnadeva Raya realized what Tenali Raman meant. He summoned the Brahmins and told them to curb their greedy nature.

Gift for a Content Man

One day Tenali Raman came to the royal court in a very cheerful mood.

He was dressed well and wore bright, shiny jewels. On seeing him, King Krishnadeva Raya said, "Tenali you look too happy today. Tell me what is the matter with you ?"

"I am no different than other days, Your Majesty," Tenali Raman said politely.

"No, you are different. When you met me the first time, you were very simple minded and humble."

Tenali Raman said, "Your Majesty, everyone changes with time especially when he has a good life and some money. I have saved much from the generous gifts you have given over the years to me."

The king said, "Then you must give and share them with others. It will make you happy."

Tenali Raman said, "Your Majesty, I have not saved enough to give yet."

"Tenali, you must build a luxurious house and gift it away to earn happiness and content in the true sense."

Tenali Raman agreed to the king's words. During the next few months he grew busy building a grand house fitted with all luxuries. As it was being built, people admired its beauty. A few months later, the luxurious house was ready. Tenali Raman then hung a board outside the house. It read, "This house is offered as a gift to a man who is happy and content with what he has."

Many people read the board but no one came to claim the house. Once a poor man from outside the city came to the house. He read it again and again. He thought that the people of this city were foolish

not to claim the house. He went to Tenali Raman and said, "Sir, I have read the board hung outside this great house. I want to claim it as I am a happy and content man. I deserve this house."

At this Tenali Raman started laughing. He said, "If you are happy and content without this house then you don't deserve this house. Because If you are content with what you have, then why do you desire for more ?"

The poor man realized his folly and left. In the royal court, Tenali Raman told his tale to the king. The king said, "I can see you have been your clever self once more. What will you do with the house ?"

"Now, I have shown you, that I can give away my things. I think I myself will move into the house on an auspicious day."

Thus, Tenali Raman proved his intelligence once again.

Tenali Raman, the Wrestler

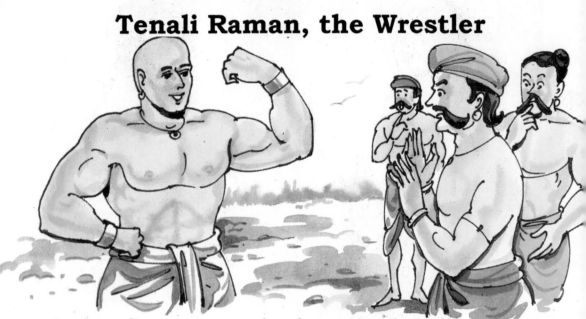

Once a famous wrestler from North India came to Vijaynagar. He had won many wrestling matches and held prestigeous titles. He challenged the wrestlers of Vijaynagar to have a wrestling match with him. His strong, tall body made the best wrestlers of Vijaynagar to backout. They went together to Tenali Raman to find a solution to the problem.

"I will fight and defeat the great wrestler from North India but you must promise to say what I ask you to. On the day of the trial of strength, you must address me as your guru. You must let me wear all the medals you have won and you must carry me on your shoulders." Tenali said to them.

The wrestlers of Vijaynagar promised this to Tenali Raman.

On the day of the trial, Tenali Raman asked the wrestlers to learn a slogan. They were to shout it loudly as they carried him on their shoulders to the arena. The slogan was, "Manmuk Maharaj ki jai ! Meese Manmuk Maharaj ki jai !"

The king and the people of Vijaynagar gathered to watch the wrestling performance. They were surprised to see thin and weak Tenali Raman being carried to the arena. He was draped with medals round his neck and the other wrestlers were shouting the slogans loudly.

The wrestler from North India thought that some great wrestler was approaching, when he heard the slogans. The slogans in Kannada were very simple. 'Manmuk' in Kannada meant to eat earth while 'Meese' also meant nearly the same. As the wrestler from North India did not understand Kannada, he thought that it was a title of the great wrestler before him.

Tenali Raman went to the wrestler and said, "Before I

start the match with you. You must tell me the meanings of the gestures I make. Every great wrestler must know these gestures. If you can tell what the gestures mean then I will fight you. If you cannot tell then you must accept defeat."

Then Tenali Raman began gesturing. He first put his right foot forward and touched the wrestler's chest with his right hand. With his left hand, he touched himself. Then placing his right hand on his left he pressed hard. Then he pointed his right index finger to the south. Then joining both his index fingers of each hand, he made a knot. Then he picked up a handful of soil and pretended to put it into his mouth.

After this, he asked the wrestler from North India to tell what the gestures meant. But the wrestler did not understand anything so he had to accept defeat. He left Vijaynagar and before leaving, gave all his medals and titles to Tenali Raman.

The king and the people of Vijaynagar were baffled by the turn of the events. The wrestlers however were very happy at winning a trial of strength without actually fighting. The king summoned Tenali Raman and asked him, "Tenali, what magic did you do through those gestures ?"

Tenali Raman said, "Your Majesty, that was no magic. It was a trick I played to befool the wrestler. The gestures I made told him that he was a strong wrestler like everyone's right hand. I was weak like everyone's left hand. If a wrestler like the right hand would challenge a weak wrestler like the left hand then the weak wrestler will be crushed like a small nut. My wife sitting in the south corner of the

arena will have to eat dirt if I lost the trial. My gestures merely gave this message to him but he did not understand at all."

Hearing this the king and the people gathered there started laughing at Tenali Raman's clever trick that chased away a strong champion wrestler.

The Baby Vessels

Once Tenali Raman received a complaint about a greedy and cheating money-lender. He used to lend money to the needy but charge ten times interest. Thus, he used to earn much more than he gave. To teach him a lesson, Tenali made a plan.

One fine morning Tenali Raman went to the money-lender's house and said, "Sir, I have heard you have three large vessels in your house. May I rent them for a day. I need them for cooking as I am hosting a feast in my house."

"Yes, surely, you may take them," the money-lender said. "But you must pay me two gold coins as rent."

Tenali Raman agreed to it. He gave the coins in advance and took the three vessels home. Then he went to the market and bought three vessels of the same shape but smaller in sizes. The next day he went to the money-lender with six vessels. He said, "Sir, here are your three large vessels. I realized that your large vessels were pregnant. They delivered these small vessels early this morning so these all belong to you."

The greedy money-lender was delighted. He had given three vessels and was getting back six vessels so he made no comments on Tenali's words. He took the six vessels from Tenali and kept them in his house.

After a few days Tenali Raman approached the money-lender once again. He said, "Sir I have a yajna to be held at my place from tomorrow. Many Brahmins and priests must be fed. I need some vessels for the large feast. I will return them after five days to you.

In a few minutes, the money-lender arranged for a cartload of large vessels. While giving them he said to Tenali, "Here is a cart full of vessels for your feast. My vessels are pregnant. You must take care of them and the young vessels they give birth to."

Tenali promised and left with the vessels. Many days went by but Tenali did not return with the vessels. The money-lender became angry. He rushed to Tenali Raman's house and said, "You had promised to return the vessels in five days but it has been a long time now. Where are they ?"

"Sir, I am sorry to inform you that they died at child birth," said Tenali.

"Oh ! You cheat ! How can you say that !" cried the money-lender.

Tenali Raman said, "Sir, perhaps you know very well that it sometimes happens that some ladies give birth to babies safely while others die at giving birth to the child ."

The money-lender said loudly, "How can they die ? How can they have babies ? You cheat, I'll take you to court for cheating me."

The argument took a serious position. None of them was ready to agree with the other. At last, the money-lender took Tenali Raman to the king for justice. In the royal court, King Krishnadeva Raya heard both

parties. Then he asked the money-lender, "You accepted the baby vessels the first time. Didn't you know that vessels don't beget babies ?"

The money-lender stood silent with a bowed head.

" If you believed Tenali earlier, then you must accept that they are dead now for only living things give birth and die."

The money-lender had nothing to say as he was filled with shame at his own greedy behaviour. Thus, Tenali Raman taught him a lesson he remembered all his life.

The King's Parrot

Once a hunter caught a pretty parrot in a jungle. He did not like killing the pretty bird so he went to the royal palace. There he gifted the parrot to King Krishnadeva Raya.

The king took to the liking of the parrot at once. A silver cage was bought for the parrot and the king himself fed it with nuts and best varieties of sweets. When the queen saw the parrot, she, too, liked it very much. Soon the royal couple were busy, taking care of the parrot. They fed the bird personally and hung its cage in their private chamber. They both taught the parrot to chant holy words. At their bidding, the parrot would say, "Hare Rama! Hare Krishna!"

One morning Tenali Raman returned from the temple after the prayers. He was wearing a silk dhoti, had a sandal mark on his forehead and held the pooja thali in his hands. He went to the king's private chamber to give him the prasad.

In the chamber, the royal couple were busy playing with the parrot. On seeing Tenali Raman, the king said, "Tenali, with your pooja thali and your sandal mark you look like a rather great devotee of God. But true devotion  is what my pet parrot shows. It can chant 'Hare Rama, Hare Krishna' when we ask it."

Then the queen asked the parrot to say and it said, "Hare Rama ! Hare Krishna ! Hare Rama ! Hare Krishna !"

To this, Tenali Raman said, "Your Majesty, this is not the parrot's devotion but the training that you have given it. You have taught it to speak those words and you reward it with tasty nuts each time it utters those words. It's merely saying so to get the nuts. But I can prove that it will not utter those words in all situations."

"Alright, go on and prove it to us," the royal couple

challenged.

Tenali Raman went out of the royal chamber. After a few minutes, he returned with a cat in his arms. On seeing the cat, the parrot grew nervous. When the cat let out a sound in pleasure, the parrot screeched in fright. The queen tried to calm the parrot and asked it to recite the holy chant but the parrot did not obey. It kept screeched as it was afraid of the cat.

Then the queen and the king realized that what they were thinking was wrong. Tenali Raman had proved his point in minutes. So the king said, "You were right, Tenali Raman. The parrot was not showing devotion."

In a disheartened tone, the queen said, "Tenali, I have no use of such a silly parrot and anyway why should we keep a parrot caged up? Let me open the cage door and set it free."

Thus, the queen set the cage door open and the parrot flew off to freedom.

Tenali Raman's Riches

Once Tenali Raman realized that king Krishnadeva Raya believed him to be a very rich man. The king thought that the rewards he gave Tenali had made him very rich. Tenali Raman wanted to clear this misunderstanding that the king had. So he made a clever plan.

One day Tenali Raman went to the royal court with a sad face. He looked very worried and nervous. King Krishnadeva Raya noticed this and enquired, "Tenali, what is worrying you ?"

"Your Majesty, a learned astrologer told me that I will die in two months time. I don't know what to do. I am not able to eat or sleep properly as I am worried about my wife and children. Who will take care of them after my death ?" said worried Tenali Raman.

The king was shocked at the news but he tried to console Tenali Raman. He said, "I cannot do anything to keep off what is written in your destiny.

Death is inevitable, but I promise to take care of your family when you breathe your last. You must stop worrying about them now."

For the next few days, Tenali Raman did not come to attend the royal court. The king grew worried and sent a messenger to find out what had happened. On his return from Tenali Raman' house, the servant told the king that Tenali Raman had high fever. The messenger was sent to Tenali Raman's house the next day, too. This time he informed the king that Tenali Raman had lost consciousness and was lying on the death bed. On the third day, the messenger reached Tenali Raman's house and found his wife and children crying loudly. His wife told the messenger, "Oh! It's misery for us now. My husband breathed his last a few hours ago. We have just returned after cremating him. Who will take care of us now?"

The messenger rushed to the king and delivered the sad news of Tenali's death to him.

"Oh! This is truly unfortunate," the king said on hearing the news. "I must make arrangements to take care of the family. Guards, go to Tenali Raman's house and ask his wife to hand over all the valuable ornaments and cash in my custody as she will now be living alone. I am afraid some robbers may rob Tenali Raman's wealth. The woman cannot keep watch on the ornaments all by herself."

Hearing these words, the guards went to Tenali Raman's house. There they met his wife and said, "Madam, the king has sent his condolences to the family. He has reassured that you and your children will be well taken care of. The king has asked you to hand over the wealth accumulated by your late husband into his safe custody. This way you won't have to fear of the wealth being stolen."

Tenali's wife was sobbing. She said,

"That big trunk in the corner is where I think my husband kept the wealth in. Please take this trunk to the king."

So, the palace guards picked the big and heavy trunk and brought it to the royal court. In the court, the king ordered the guards to open the trunk. The guards promptly obeyed their king. When the trunk's lid was opened, there was a collective gasp in the court. Out of the trunk emerged Tenali Raman himself. He was alive and not dead as he had made everyone believe. The king was also shocked to see Tenali in flesh.

Tenali bowed low to the king. The king asked in a surprised tone, "Tenali, what a surprise ! You are alive ! Then why did you make us think that you were no more ?"

"Your Majesty, I wanted to show you that this

trunk did not have wealth in it as you thought. It merely had me in it. My intelligence and wit is my true wealth."

"But what about all the rich rewards I have given you through the years."

"Your Majesty, I never developed the habit of hoarding money. I always use the amount I need and the rest I always give away as alms to the poor and the needy."

Hearing these words, King Krishnadeva Raya felt that he had been wrong in thinking this way about Tenali Raman. He was glad that he had been put right by the intelligent plan made by Tenali Raman.

Tenali Raman, the Painter

Once a painter visited King Krishnadeva Raya's court. He gifted a painting to the king. The painting was that of a deer. The king liked the painting very much and decided to keep it. He showed it to a minister. The minister also admired the painter's skill. Then the king wanted to get Tenali Raman's opinion about the painting, so he summoned him and handed over the painting to him. Tenali Raman took the painting. He started examining it with a keen eye. Some moments later, the king asked him, "Tenali, what is wrong? Why are you looking so seriously at the painting? Do you see anything mysterious in this painting? If so, ask the painter. He will satisfy you."

"Your Majesty, as far as my knowledge goes, every deer is gifted with two ears. In this painting I see the deer has only one ear."

Hearing Tenali Raman's comment, the painter went near to Tenali Raman and looked at the painting. He saw that what Tenali Raman was saying was true. One of the ears of the deer was missing. But the painter thought that if he accepted his fault, he would be insulted in the royal court. He was afraid the king might scold him for gifting an incomplete painting. To hide his fault, the painter made an excuse. He said, "Your Majesty, this painting of mine is symbolic in nature. You can see that the deer is looking at a place on the far right, thus, its right ear has been obscured. Only one, having a keen knowledge of paintings, can understand the meaning of this work."

Tenali Raman felt let down by these words. But he decided to prove his point, so he said, "The great painter is correct. I am no critic of art having the knowledge of these points. Tomorrow I'll present a painting made by me to prove this."

The next day Tenali Raman arrived in the royal

court carrying two paintings. He hung them on a wall and covered both with clothes. On the king's arrival, the minister and the painter also accompanied him. The threesome then went to see Tenali Raman's painting. With a grand movement of his hands, Tenali unveiled his works of art. The king was surprised on seeing the paintings. The minister and the painter also could make no sense of them. One painting was that of a horse. But the parts of the horse's body were drawn separately all over the canvas. It was not a painting of a horse in one piece. The second painting was that of a horse rider. A corner of the canvas had the rider's hands, the other corner had his head and so on. This really baffled the king, the minister and the painter.

"So, do you admire the picture of a rider on a horse ?" asked Tenali. But the three of them shook their head for they had not made any sense of his work of art. So Tenali Raman explained, "The horse is painted in one picture and the rider in the other. Looking at them together, they present the whole picture of a horse rider, don't you see ?"

The painter realized that Tenali Raman was pointing out his folly indirectly. He realized his mistake and stepped forward. He bowed low to the king and said, "Your Majesty, please forgive me. My painting really had a mistake in it. I was scared of being insulted, so I tried to hide my mistake by a false explanation."

The king understood what Tenali Raman had

brought to light. He rewarded the painter for his skill and honesty and Tenali Raman received an award for bringing the mistake to light.

The Gift of Elephants

As is well known, King Krishnadeva Raya used to give handsome rewards to Tenali Raman on several occasions. Once pleased by Tenali Raman, the king gifted him five elephants. Being a poor man, Tenali Raman could not afford to take care of those huge animals. They needed a lot of food to eat. Tenali Raman could not even feed his own family very well and the burden of feeding five large elephants was just too much for him. But without protesting much he accepted the royal gifts and took the elephants home.

At home, Tenali Raman's wife started complaining, "We can't even feed ourselves properly. Where will we get money for their food ? We cannot even pay to keep a care-taker for these animals. If the king had gifted us five cows instead of five elephants, atleast we could have used their milk for the children or to make butter and curd to feed ourselves."

Tenali Raman realized that his wife was correct but he had no excuse to give, so he got up and said, "I'll be back soon. I want to first dedicate these elephants to the name of Goddess Kali."

So, Tenali led the elephants to the Kali temple, and put the seal of Goddess Kali on their foreheads. Then he set them free to roam around the city. Some kind-hearted citizens felt pity and fed the elephants. But most of the times the elephants went hungry. Soon they  became weak and frail. Someone told about the elephants' plight to the king. The king became angry at once at the way Tenali Raman had treated the elephants. So he summoned Tenali Raman to the royal court and asked him, "Tenali Raman, why did you treat those elephants so harshly ?"

"Your Highness, when you rewarded me with the five elephants, I could not refuse, for it would have meant going against the royal wish. But I being a poor man, could not take the extra burden of caring the elephants, while I was already having such a large family to feed. If Your Majesty would have gifted me with five cows instead of these five elephants, atleast I would have benefitted from them."

The king realized his mistake and said, "Will you mistreat the cows if I gave them to you ?"

"No, Your Majesty, cows are sacred creatures. Moreover, the milk from the cows will be fed to my children and they'll always thank you for such a useful royal gift."

So, the king ordered the guards to keep the elephants in the royal sheds and five cows were given as reward to Tenali Raman to take home for his family.

Tenali Raman the Obedient Servant

Once King Krishnadeva Raya asked Tenali Raman to accompany him. The king was going to give away gems and pearls as alms to the Brahmins. The king mounted on a horse. Two bags-full of pearls and gems were placed on horse-back, too. Then the king said, "Tenali, follow me, walking behind the horse. You must see if any pearls or gems fall out of the bags."

So as the king proceeded on horse-back, Tenali followed him on foot. After some time, the heavy bags could not take the weight of the gems and pearls. A small split opened in the bag and the pearls and gems fell on the ground. But as Tenali was told to see if anything fell and not to tell about it, so he did not say anything to the king.

As they proceeded, they passed by a lake. The king got off the horse and sat down to rest. Then he thought of taking a dip in the cool lake waters. So he took off his clothes and gave them to Tenali

Raman for safe keep. As the king got into the waters he started chanting aloud, "Hare Rama ! Hare Krishna !"

In Kannada, 'Hare' means 'to tear' and since Tenali Raman's full name was Tenali Ramakrishna, he thought that the king was asking him to tear something. As he had nothing but the king's clothes, so he tore them to pieces.

A while later the king came out of the lake water and asked for his clothes. At this, Tenali Raman offered him his own clothes. When the king asked why he was doing so, Tenali Raman replied, "I merely obeyed your order, Your Majesty. You asked me to 'hare' so I tore the clothes just as I had watched the gems and pearls falling as you had asked me to."

The king first laughed heartily. Then he realized that giving incomplete order was wrong and in his own way Tenali Raman had taught him another lesson that he was giving his wealth away uselessly, where it was not necessary at all.

True Beauty

Once King Krishnadeva Raya ordered that his kingdom must be well maintained and decorated. He wanted to make Vijaynagar as beautiful as heaven on Earth. Many famous and skilled architects, sculptors and gardeners worked hard to make the capital city a beautiful place. The king wanted every foreign visitor to describe the beauty of the vijaynagar to the people of their land. The most beautiful temples and well-planned forts and fortresses were soon created. Soon the fame of the beautiful city spread far and wide as the king had wished for. Many travellers and tourists came to enjoy the beauty of Vijaynagar. The king was really very happy.

One day the king sat in the Royal Court surrounded by his courtiers and ministers. Everyone was discussing the successful work of beautifying the city. The king was praising the workers and the ministers who had laboured hard to get such fine results. Tenali Raman was also present in the court but he was not taking interest in that discussion.

A jealous minister got a golden chance to get Tenali Raman into trouble. He said, "Your Majesty, it seems Tenali Raman is not happy by the fame we have earned by beautifying the kingdom. "By his quite self it seems that he has a grudge against your happiness."

The comment angered the king. He turned to Tenali Raman furiously and enquired, "Tenali, is it true ? Are you not happy to see the fame and prosperity of my kingdom ? Is Vijaynagar not beautiful enough for you ?"

At this Tenali Raman said, "Your Majesty, the city has been beautified but.."

"Yes, yes! Complete your sentence. But what?"

"But, Your Majesty, there is one thing that you have overlooked."

"And what have I overlooked, will you tell me frankly.?" asked the king.

"For that you need to accompany me, Your Majesty." The king agreed and went with Tenali Raman. He led the king to the outskirts of the city. Many slums were there. Most of the labourers and craftsmen who had worked to make Vijaynagar beautiful used to stay there. The houses there did not have water or drainage systems. Many people were paying money as royal tax even though they did not have enough to eat. The poor conditions of the people really disheartened the king. On seeing the king, many people gathered around him and started making complaints. The king heard all of them and promised to solve the problems.

On his return to the royal palace, king Krishnadeva Raya said to Tenali Raman, "You were right, Tenali. Thank you for opening my eyes to the plight of my people. What is the use of a beautiful well maintained city when its citizens are not happy ? I must cancel all the taxes imposed on the people for bearing the expenses of beautifying the city. What is the use of all this if I cannot make my people's life comfortable and beautiful ?"

Thus, Tenali Raman served not only as a jester but as a critic for the king too.

The Winter Penance

Once a priest wanted to cheat King Krishnadeva Raya by misusing the king's generous nature. He went to the king and said, "Your Majesty, these are the cold days of winter yet, to clean Vijaynagar of evil spirits, I want to perform a difficult penance. Everyday, I'll stand in the cold water of the Tungbhadra river before sunrise. After sunrise, I will perform the yajna whose holy smoke will clean the atmosphere of the city of all the evil spirits."

For this, the priest asked for one lakh gold coins. The king gave the amount generously. The priest started the penance from next morning itself. Every morning before sunrise he used to stand in waist deep water of the river Tungbhadra. As it was very cold, people used to wonder how the priest could stand in such a cold water for so long. Thus, everyday many people used to gather on the

banks of the river to see the priest. When some days went by, the king also felt the desire to see the priest as he performed the penance. Next morning King Krishnadeva Raya and Tenali Raman left for the riverside. They saw a large crowd on the riverside. Everyone was wearing warm clothes yet their teeth were clattering in the cold. But the priest was standing in the cold water effortlessly. Tenali Raman was sure that the priest was up to some tricks to befool the people. He went nearer the river but the royal guard didn't allow him to meet the priest. They said, "Sir, the priest has asked us not to let anyone near the water or in the water during the penance. If someone goes near him, the penance would not complete."

Hearing this Tenali Raman was even more sure that the priest has made up some plan to befool the people. To unveil the priest's tricks, Tenali Raman said, "Your Majesty, it has been a long time now. Let me help the priest come out of the cold water."

"Yes, indeed. Call him ashore. I want to talk to him."

So Tenali Raman went into the water and approached the priest. He greeted him and pulled him by the hand to get him ashore. But the priest did not move. At this, Tenali Raman pulled harder but the priest looked nervous and did not move. Then Tenali Raman said to the king, "Your Majesty, I think the priest's legs have got cramped due to the cold water."

The priest did not say anything as the king was watching. This time, when Tenali Raman pulled him, the priest walked ashore from the water. He could not think of being punished by the king if he refused to meet him. When he came to the shore his white dhoti had turned blue. The king exclaimed, "Oh, Tenali Raman ! Look at the poor priest's legs. They have turned blue due to the cold cramp."

Tenali Raman smiled at the king and said, "No, Your Majesty, you are wrong. Actually the priest was wearing warm water proof garments under his dhoti so that his feet and legs did not get cold in the water. The poor quality garments have lost their blue colour which has stained the priest's dhoti."

Hearing this explanation, the king laughed at first at the funny situation. Now he knew why the priest did not want to come out of the water. Then he scolded the priest for lying to him. The king claimed back the money given for the penance and yajna and asked the priest to leave Vijaynagar forever.

The Telltale Nails

Everyone knew that King Krishnadeva Raya was greatly fond of birds and animals. One day a bird-catcher came to the king in the royal court. He had a beautiful, colourful yet strange looking bird in a cage. He bowed low to the king and said, "Your Majesty, I caught this strange and beautiful rare bird in the forest yesterday. It can sing sweetly and can also talk like a parrot. It is not only colourful like the peacock but it can also dance like one. I have come to sell this bird to you."

The king saw the beautiful bird and said, "Yes, this bird does look rare and colourful. You'll be suitably rewarded for this."

The king ordered the treasurer to give the bird-catcher fifty gold coins and keep the bird in the palace garden. But just then Tenali Raman got up from his seat and said, "Your Majesty, I don't think this bird can dance like a peacock in the rain. In fact I feel the bird has not taken a bath for many years. Let me prove it to you."

With these words, Tenali Raman picked a glass of water and poured it on the bird in the cage. The bird got drenched and suddenly all the courtiers looked at the bird in surprise. The water flowing off the bird's body was coloured and the bird appeared to be of light brown colour. The king  looked at Tenali Raman in surprise. Tenali Raman said, "Your Majesty, this is no rare, colourful bird. It is an ordinary wild pigeon of the woods."

"But, Tenali, how did you realize that this bird had been dyed in false colours ?"

"From the bird-catchers coloured nails, Your Majesty. The colours he used to paint the bird are still present on his nails and fingers."

Hearing these comments the bird-catcher tried to run away from the court. But the guards caught him. He was put in prison. The reward to be given to him was then given to Tenali Raman by the king. Thus, Tenali Raman's attentive nature saved the king's wealth once again.

The Magical Wells

Once King Krishnadeva Raya ordered his Home Minister to build many wells around his kingdom. Summer was nearing and the king wanted the wells to be dug, so that his people did not suffer in the summer heat. The Home Minister took a large sum of money from the treasury for the task. Soon it was reported that many wells had been dug as the king had ordered. The king went around the city and inspected some, himself. He was satisfied that his orders had been carried out well.

One day in summer, some villagers from outside the capital city came to meet Tenali Raman. They had some complaint against the Home Minister. Tenali Raman heard their complaint and told them how to seek justice for it. According to the plan, the next day Tenali Raman addressed the king. He said, "Your Majesty, I have news about some strange thiefs in Vijaynagar. They have been stealing our wells."

At this King Krishnadeva Raya said, "Don't be ridiculous, Tenali. How can one steal a well ?"

"Your Majesty! I was sure that you would not believe me, so I have brought some villagers with me. They are waiting outside the royal court.

If you do not believe me, please allow them to come to the court. They will give you the details of the matter."

The king allowed the villagers to come to the court. One of the villagers said, "Your Majesty, the wells dug and built by the Home Minister have vanished. You can come and see for yourself."

The king agreed. Accompanied by the Home

Minister, Tenali Raman, some courtiers and the villagers, the king went to inspect the wells. On inspecting all over the kingdom he observed that the capital city and the bordering villages had enough good wells but the villages far away from the capital had no wells at all.

The Home Minister grew nervous. Actually he had ordered for only some wells to be built. The money for the others had been spent by him on luxuries. When the king turned to the Home Minister in anger, Tenali Raman intervened. He said, "Your Majesty, its not his fault. Actually, they were magical wells. They vanished into thin air a few days after being built."

The king realized what had occurred. He scolded the Home Minister strongly. He was ordered to build a hundred more wells for which he had to pay from his own pocket. Tenali Raman was given the responsibility of looking over the job.

Babapur's Ramlila

Every year a drama troupe from Kashi used to visit Vijaynagar before Dussehra. They used to perform Ramlila for the king and the citizens of Vijaynagar. But one year the king got the message that the drama troupe from Kashi would not arrive at all this time. The reason was that the many members of the drama troupe had taken ill. King Krishnadeva Raya felt disheartened. The Ramlila performance was an old custom of Vijaynagar and everyone used to look forward to it.

The Rajguru said, "Your Majesty, I can send a message to call the artists from Rampur."

"But it will take some weeks for them to reach here," the king said.

At this, Tenali Raman suggested, "Your Majesty, I know a troupe from nearby. They can be here in two days and will give a fine Ramlila performance."

The king agreed and felt happy. Soon the whole arrangements were made for the Ramlila performance. The Ramlila Ground was cleared and

cleaned. The large stage was set up. The city was decorated for the Navratras. The people were excited as always to watch the Ramlila. A small fair was held near the place, where the Ramlila was to be performed. In a few days, the troupe was ready for the performance. The king, the courtiers, the ministers and the people, everyone watched the Ramlila every night of the Navratras. The last episode on Dussehra was admired by all. Most of the troupe members were children. Their sensitive and impressive acting brought tears in the eyes of the people.

After Dussehra, the king invited some ministers and the drama troupe members for a grand feast at the royal palace. After the feast, the king rewarded the troupe members for their great performance.

Then he asked Tenali Raman, "Where did you get such great performers Tenali ? Where has this Ramlila troupe come from ?"

"From Babapur, Your Majesty," Tenali Raman replied.

"Babapur ? Where is Babapur in our kingdom ? I have not heard about it before," asked the king surprisingly.

"It's near Vijaynagar, Your Majesty," Tenali replied.

But a small boy who was member of the drama troupe spoke up, "Your Majesty, we are from Vijaynagar. Baba Tenali Raman trained us to do the play in three days time. That's why we call it Babapur's Ramlila."

At this the king burst out laughing. He rewarded Tenali for the skilful training of the drama troupe.

The Sick Horses

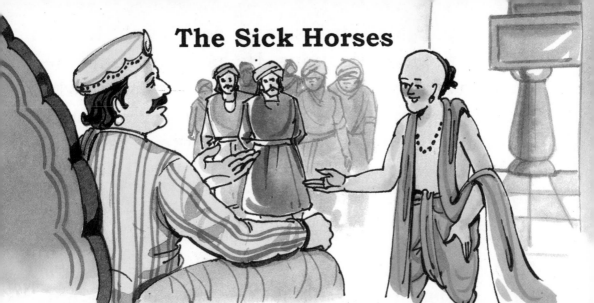

Once an unknown disease struck the horses in Vijaynagar. There was panic all around the city. The people who owned expensive and well-breed horses, started to sell them at a very low cost. This happened so because it came to be known that the horses were dying of the unknown disease and it was also spreading to the people who came in contact with the horses. Many people and soldiers who owned horses sold them.

King Krishnadeva Raya also heard about this. He asked his servants to take special care of the horses in the royal stables. But a servant said, "Your Majesty, it's amazing but the horses in the royal stables are in perfect health."

The king grew confused and summoned Tenali Raman. He said, "Tenali Raman, the horses in the kingdom are being sold for fear of some disease. But I am surprised to know that the horses in the royal stables are healthy. I want you to investigate about it."

"Yes, Your Majesty" saying so, Tenali Raman started the investigations. He assigned some men to roam around the city and find some clue to what was happening. A few days later, his men caught some men and brought them to the royal court. The men were asked by the king, "What were you doing when you were caught ?"

"Your Majesty, we were talking about sick horses."

"Have you seen some sick horse ?" asked the king. One of them replied, "No, Your Majesty. We have not seen any sick horse. We have only heard about them."

The king realized at once that someone had spread the rumour of sick horses and no disease had affected the horses. The king did not know how to stop the rumours. Tenali Raman saw how worried the king looked. He asked his men to be alert once again.

Two days later, Tenali Raman presented a man and a woman in the royal court. He told the king, "Your Majesty, I had asked my people to go around the city and be alert. They caught this couple. They belong to the neighbouring kingdom."

At this, the king turned to the couple in anger and asked, "What are you doing in my kingdom?"

"I'll tell you, Your Majesty," Tenali Raman insisted. "The king of our neighbouring kingdom had sent them here to spread the rumour of sick horses. This way the people of our kingdom would sell their horses at low cost. These horses were bought by these spies at low cost to be used in their royal cavalry. On the other hand, our soldiers and warriors were disheartened and lost confidence in themselves. Our kingdom has the best soldiers and the best horses making up our cavalry. Lack of confidence and morale would make our soldiers weak. Thus, when the neighbouring king attacks us, he would surely win."

"Oh! such a dangerous plan !" exclaimed the king.

The king ordered the spies to be executed the next day. He announced that no one was to sell their horses due to false rumours. Then the king thanked Tenali Raman for his investigative plan. He rewarded Tenali Raman and his men for their efforts.

The Colourful Sweets

Once a royal order was given that the kingdom of Vijaynagar would celebrate the national festival. The city was cleaned up. Lightings were put up on buildings and street poles. Flowers adorned the palace and house gates. Throughout the capital, people were in a festive mood.

King Krishnadeva Raya announced, "To celebrate the national festival, the sweet shops must sell colourful sweets. They will be attractive to look at and good to eat."

After the announcement, the sweet shop owners also got busy in making colourful sweets.

For some days, Tenali Raman was not seen in the royal court. The king sent guards to search for him and bring him to the court but they could not find him. They went to the court and told this to the king. The king grew worried and asked the guards to search more carefully. After some more days the guards found Tenali Raman. They went and informed the king, "Your Majesty, we have found Tenali Raman. He has opened a shop of colour dyes and spends the whole day dyeing people's clothes. When we asked him to accompany us, he refused to come with us."

At this the king grew furious. He said to the guards, "I order you to bring Tenali Raman here as soon as possible. If he does not come with you, bring him forcefully."

So the guards obeyed the king's orders and fetched Tenali Raman forcefully.

Thus, he was brought to the royal court. The king enquired, "Tenali, how could you refuse the royal orders when I sent the guards to fetch you ? And what has made you open this colour dye shop ? You have a good position in the royal court which takes care of all your needs."

Tenali Raman said, "Your Majesty, I wanted

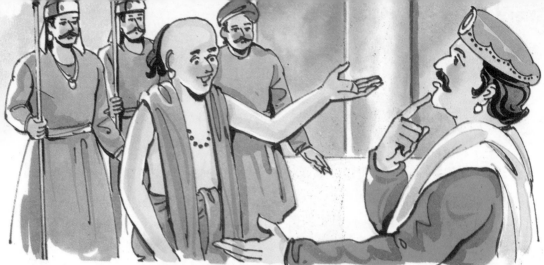

to dye my clothes for the national festival. I wanted to complete the dyeing quickly before all the colour was used up."

"Why do you think that all the colour dye would be used up ? Is everyone upto dyeing their clothes ?"

"No, Your Majesty. Actually after your orders for preparing colourful sweets, the sweet shop owners are busy buying the colour dyes for dyeing sweets. If they buy all of the dyes to be put in the sweets then how can I dye my clothes."

At this the king realized his mistake. He said, "So you are trying to tell me that following my orders as excuse, the sweet shop owners are using cheap, harmful cloth dyes in their sweets. Even though they must use the permitted food colours only. I hereby take back the orders for colourful sweets. Those sweet shop owners who have used the harmful chemical dyes in sweets will be severely punished."

Thus, once again Tenali Raman saved the lives of people of Vijaynagar through an intelligent plan.

The Theft

Once a very skilled painter arrived in the royal court of Vijaynagar. The king and the courtiers were very impressed by his colourful paintings. They were very beautiful indeed. King Krishnadeva Raya ordered the painter to make his portrait. In a few days' time, the portrait was ready and everyone admired it. Then, impressed by his skill, the king allowed the painter to make detailed pictures of the royal palace. The painter expressed his wish to roam around the whole palace for observation of every corner from inside and outside the palace. With this permission granted, the painter was now free to roam around the fort and the palace. So now, one could see the painter in various chambers of the palace during the day.

A few days went by. Now the painter was ready with the detailed pictures of the royal palace. He presented the pictures of palace to the king. The colourful, detailed pictures were perfect. The courtiers were also impressed by the beauty of the pictures. After seeing the pictures, the king said, "I am very happy to see your beautiful paintings. I wish you to stay as our royal guest for two more days. In the meantime I will honour you in a public function and give you many rewards."

The painter agreed to stay there for two more days. Then, arrangements were made for a large gathering in a public function. At the function, the painter was felicitated with many precious gifts, medals and flowers. After the function, the painter went to his room and rested. Next morning he was scheduled to leave. But lo ! When he got up the next day, his paintings and painting materials were missing. Someone had stolen them. The painter rushed to the royal court to complain about the theft.

In the royal court, the king was sitting with his courtiers. The painter went to the court and told about his missing belongings to the king. Just when the king was about to call the guards to search for the thief, Tenali Raman got up from his seat and said, "Your Majesty, there is no need to look for the thief. I know who the thief is."

"Tenali, if you know the thief, why don't you tell us about him ?"

"Your Majesty, I am the thief."

"Tenali Raman, you a thief ! What do you mean by all this ?"

"Your Majesty, I stole the painter's belongings and here is the reason for it. When the painter had begun impressing you, I became suspicious about his intentions. I sent my men to investigate. The investigations have revealed that this man is a spy from our enemy. He had posed as a painter to know the detailed entries and exits of our royal palace and fort. When he painted the picture of the palace, he drew a map of the entries and exits of the palace and fort also. The belongings I stole contain the map also. I had stolen them to stop him from leaving the kingdom."

Hearing this, the king was both shocked and angry. He ordered the guards to put the painter immediately in prison and took back all the awards and rewards given to him. Thus, Tenali Raman again protected the Vijaynagar kingdom from destruction.

Meeting the Fairies

Once a visitor came to the royal court of Vijaynagar and wished to meet king Krishnadeva Raya. One of the guards informed the king about his arrival. The king permitted the visitor to meet him.

The visitor was very tall and thin man. He was blue bodied. Standing straight before the king, he said, "Your Majesty, I am Neelketu from Neeldesh. I have knowledge of the place where the fairies reside. I can summon the fairies in your presence through the magical powers I possess."

The king grew excited on hearing these words. He said, "Tell me Neelketu, what do I need to do for this."

Neelketu replied, "Your Majesty, all you have to do is come to the old tank of water just outside the city. You will have to come there tonight at midnight and you must come all alone. Then I'll summon the fairies to dance for you."

The king agreed to this. That night the king took his horse and rode to the old tank outside the city. The tank was a large and old water storage area with a ruined fort surrounding it. When the king reached the old tank, Neelketu emerged from the ruins of the forts. He said, "Welcome, Your Majesty, I have made the arrangements. I have already called the fairies. They are inside there, where the courtyard of the ruined fort is. They will soon dance for you."

The king got down from the horse to go in with Neelketu. Just as he stepped forward, they heard the sound of a clap. Suddenly, they were surrounded by soldiers from the Vijaynagar army. The king was taken by surprise. The soldiers at once rushed towards Neelketu and caught him and put him in hand cuffs.

"What's all this ? What's going on ?" The king enquired in surprise.

Just then Tenali Raman appeared from behind a tree. He said, "Your Majesty, I'll tell you what is going on. This man is a minister of defence from our neighbouring kingdom. Inside the ruined fort, there are no fairies waiting to dance for you. Actually, the soldiers from his kingdom are hiding there, dressed as fairies. The false wings they have, have hidden weapons in them. Their plan was to kill you by surrounding you. But I came to know of it."

"Tenali Raman, I thank you once again for saving my life. But tell me how did you find this out ?"

Tenali Raman said, "Your Majesty, when Neelketu came to the court, he had painted his body with blue paint to show you that he was from Neeldesh. But when he knew that the royal court of Vijaynagar is full of intelligent and learned persons, he became nervous. He feared that he may be caught so he started sweating. The streaks of sweat on his forehead had swept away the paint at some places and his true skin colour was showing. My suspicion had been aroused. I sent my servants to follow him. They saw him talking to his soldiers as they discussed your murder's plan."

The king was impressed by Tenali Raman's alert mind and thanked him again. Then they both returned to the royal palace followed by their soldiers and the prisoners.

The Tricoloured Flowers

It was King Krishnadeva Raya's birthday. The whole kingdom was decorated with flowers and lightings. Festoons and feasts were being seen all around. Poor people and Brahmins were given food and clothes.

As usual a dance and drama festival was held in the royal court. A feast had also been arranged for the courtiers, ministers and close friends of the King. There was gaiety and festivity all around. Then it was time for the ministers and courtiers to give gifts to the king on the grand occasion. Many expensive gifts were given to the king. Some gave gems and jewels, some gave silk from foreign lands, others gave rare antiques. But, inspite of all this, the king did not look happy. It seemed that none of the gifts was pleasing him, so he looked unhappy. Just then a courtier noticed that amongst all the people present in the court, Tenali Raman was missing. He got a chance to say something against Tenali Raman. The courtier was always jealous of Tenali Raman's importance in the court. He said to the king, "Your Majesty, please accept my congratulations and best wishes on your birthday. I see that everyone is happily greeting you and enjoying the festivities but I cannot see Tenali Raman anywhere; may be he is showing his miser nature. He did not come to wish you on your birthday for fear of spending on some expensive gift for you."

These words really made the king angry. He was also worried by Tenali Raman's absence and the courtier's words were like fuel in the fire. But still the king remained calm.

A few hours later, just when everyone had finished presenting their gifts to the king,

Tenali Raman arrived in the royal court. He bowed low to the king and said, "Your Majesty, my best wishes to you on your birthday."

"Thank you, Tenali Raman, but where have you been all this time ?"

"Your Majesty, I was busy getting a valuable gift for you." Tenali said.

With these words, Tenali Raman handed over a large packet to the king. The king put his hand in the packet and pulled out a pot. The pot had tricoloured flower plant planted in it. The king's face lit up with happiness and surprise. He said, "Tenali Raman, how did you know that I wished to get these flowers some how ? I've been yearning to see them."

The flowers were indeed very beautiful. They had purple, red and blue patched petals. They almost looked like the soft colourful wings of a butterfly. The king took the flower pot and set it beside his throne on a small table. He kept admiring it with a smile on his face. Then he looked at Tenali Raman again. Tenali Raman said, "Your Majesty, you may recall that last month we had gone to the forest of Paharpur valley for a hunting trip. We had seen these flowers growing in that forest. You had been so fascinated by their beauty that you had kept wandering around these plants for long time. When you had asked one of the guards about the plant, I knew that you wished it to grew in your garden. So, I thought of fulfilling your wish on your birthday. I got late because I had gone to Paharpur to get these plants for you."

Hearing this, the king's heart was filled with great joy. He said, "Tenali Raman, you have made me very happy today. Your sincerity towards me and the true feelings for me are evident by this gift you have given. This simple gift given from your heart is more precious to me than all the extravagant and expensive gifts."

When he said these words, Tenali Raman bowed humbly. The other courtiers who had given expensive gifts stood speechless as they watched the scene.

The Moonlit Forest

One day Tenali Raman said to the King Krishnadeva Raya, "Your Majesty, it is autumn now. Tonight is a full moon night. I have many a times enjoyed horse riding or walking on a moonlit autumn night. Will you accompany me tonight ?".

"Yes, Tenali why not ?" Said the king.

That night the king, the Prime Minister, Tenali Raman and some guards left to enjoy a moonlit night. A cool breeze was blowing slowly. The night seemed draped in silver silk as the full moon shed its light all around. The king was enjoying himself. Tenali Raman said, "Your Majesty, we are still in the city. If you permit, we can proceed to the forest on the outskirts of the city. There you can see the beauty of nature draped in moonlight."

The king agreed and the group proceeded to the forest. Tenali Raman's words had been true. The plants and trees in the forest were truly looking magnificent in the moonlight. The king relaxed and took pleasure in the sights of nature. Just then he heard the voices of some people.

"Who can be here' in the forest so late in the night ?" The king asked. But all the companions were surprised and frightened. No one could answer the question asked by the king.

Then they saw a row of bullock carts coming down the path. Some people sat driving the carts which were loaded with timber. The king asked, "What is this ? Where are you taking these logs of wood ?"

One of the bullock-cart drivers got down and approached the king. He said, "Your Majesty, these logs have been gained by cutting the trees in these forests. These belong to Seth Hiramal. We are taking it to the river. These logs will be put into the boats. Then, with the boats, these logs will float downward to the capital city of our neighbouring kingdom. There, these logs will be collected. Seth Hiramal sells these logs at twice the price to our neighbours."

The king was furious to hear this. He said, "Call Seth Hiramal immediately. He cannot carry on this illegal task. This is smuggling of wood."

The bullock-cart driver said, "Your Majesty, if you go down to the bank of the river, you can find Seth Hiramal."

The king became very angry. He rode quickly to the bank of the river. The others also followed him. Sure enough Seth Hiramal stood there with some men. He was waiting with some boatmen for the bullock-carts to arrive. On seeing the king and his men, Seth Hiramal grew nervous. The king said, "Seth Hiramal, we have come to know all about your wood smuggling. I am

going to punish you."

Then the king turned to his Prime Minister and said, "Ask your men to enquire into the matter and get all the details. This man must be punished severely for what he has done."

At this Tenali Raman intervened and said, "Your Majesty, I think the person who helps Seth Hiramal must also be punished."

"Surely, surely ! Name his associate Tenali." Tenali Raman said, "I think you should ask Seth Hiramal himself."

"Tell me who assists you in all this ?" The king asked Seth Hiramal.

Seth Hiramal became very nervous. He started sweating and could barely speak. Seeing this, Tenali Raman intervened. He said, "Your Majesty, Seth Hiramal's assistant is our own honourable Prime Minister. He is the one who gave him the idea and the permission to carry out this plan. For overlooking this smuggling, seth Hiramal pays the

Prime Minister five hundred gold coins each week."

The king turned to the Prime Minister with anger. The Prime Minister stood shamefaced and was pale with fright. The king said, "Shame on you. Being a Prime Minister you hold a prestigious position in our kingdom. Your good conduct must set an example for others but you are taking bribes. Thereby I dismiss you from this job."

The guards took Seth Hiramal and the Prime Minister in custody.

Then Tenali Raman said, "Your Majesty, I lied to you about enjoying moonlit autumn nights. Actually, I had no proof to prove what was going on, so I brought you here to the scene of the crime. Sorry for I have troubled you."

The King smiled and said, "No Tenali Raman. It was no trouble at all. In fact it has truly been an enjoyable night which I will remember all my life."

The Value of Freedom

Once a foreign visitor came to Vijaynagar. He went to meet king Krishnadeva Raya in the royal court. He bowed low to the king and said, "Your Majesty, I have heard much about your prosperous kingdom. Your just and generous nature is appreciated worldwide. I have also been heard of your wise ministers. Now I want to pose a question to them to test them ?"

The king said, "You are welcome to ask any question you want to ?"

Then the foreign visitor said, "Your Majesty, can anyone answer which is the most valuable thing of your kingdom ? The one who gives me the best answer will get this beautiful diamond necklace that I have brought as a reward."

The king looked at his wise ministers to see who

would answer and win the reward. A minister got up and named 'the royal treasure' as the most valuable thing. Another named 'the king's gem-studded crown'. Another one named 'the luxurious palace' as a valuable thing. All through this answering session, Tenali Raman had not said a word. The king said, "Tenali Raman, why have you not answered the question yet ?"

"I was about to answer, Your Majesty."

"So what is your answer to the question posed by our honoured guest ?"

Tenali Raman turned to the foreign visitor and said, "Respected sir, I think the most valuable thing in our kingdom is freedom. The people are nobody's slaves. They lead a free and happy life."

"Well, Tenali Raman, you will have to prove it to me. Can you do it ?" The visitor asked.

"Yes, surely, sir. Give me a few days time."

"Yes," said the king, "Till then you will be our special guest. Tenali Raman will see to the arrangements made for your comfortable stay in the royal guest-house."

Thus, the foreign visitor moved to the royal guest-house. Tenali Raman provided him with a large variety of dishes to choose from. His bed was soft and covered with silk blankets and sheets. Maids and servants were at the beck and call of the visitor. Singers and dancers were deployed to provide great entertainment.

For the first two days, the visitor enjoyed all the luxurious facilities provided to him. On the third day, he felt like taking a stroll by the riverside, so he went out of the royal guest house. But before he could reach the gates, the guards stopped him. They said, "Sir, we have orders not to let you go out of here."

The visitor was surprised but he agreed thinking that it may be because of his personal safety. The next evening,

he got bored and wanted to go out again. The guards stopped him yet again. This time the visitor got irritated. This went on for seven days. All the facilities were given to the visitor to enjoy but he was not allowed to go outside. Every time he tried to go outside, the guards stopped him. He felt imprisoned. Soon he stopped enjoying in the guest house. He always looked sullen (obstinate) and lost his temper for even a small mistake of the servants.

Fifteen days went by. Then the king summoned the visitor to the royal court. He asked, "Sir, how are you ? Have you enjoyed a pleasant stay in our hospitable kingdom ?"

The visitor grew furious, "How can you ask me this question ? Can't you see my condition ? I am feeling miserable and I have not shaven or had any food for days. I might as well be dead ?"

"What are you saying, sir ?" the king asked. "Didn't Tenali Raman make good arrangements in the royal guest-house ?"

"The arrangements were made very well, but I did not enjoy them. This was because I was like a prisoner in a luxurious house. The guards did not let me go out even once during the last fifteen days."

When the king asked the guards, they said, "Your Majesty, we were merely following Tenali Raman's orders."

The king turned to Tenali Raman in anger and said, "Tenali, is this how you treat an honourable guest ?"

"Your Majesty, I was merely doing what the visitor had asked me to. He wanted me to prove that freedom is the most valuable thing in Vijaynagar. By not letting him go out of the guest-house, I had taken away his freedom. See, how he is reacting to lack of freedom. I have merely proved my point."

At this, the king smiled. The foreign visitor said, "Indeed, I am impressed. You have proved your point. Now you can take this diamond necklace as your reward."

Tenali Raman bowed low and accepted the reward. Then he apologised to the visitor for having treated him harshly. The foreign visitor forgave him with a smile.